Thumbfishing
for People

My First Hitchhiking Adventure

By Clark Fitzgerald

PublishAmerica
Baltimore

ISBN: 1-60474-005-1
PUBLISHED BY PUBLISHAMERICA, LLLP
www.publishamerica.com
Baltimore

Printed in the United States of America

For everyone who picks me up!

And special thanks to my Grandpa John Robinson, who continues to inspire me. I'm always grateful to my parents, and all the rest of my family. Also I'll give a shout out to Alpha Company, 37th Engineers—Outlaws!

Thumbfishing for People

My First Hitchhiking Adventure

Introduction

Just stand on the side of the road, stick out your thumb, and wait. That's all you have to do. The simplicity of this humble enterprise confuses people. Various circumstances help improve your odds, such as smiling, being highly visible, looking clean cut, standing where a driver can pull over, etc, etc.

For a long time, I've been itching to do something. What that something was I couldn't ever really put my finger on, but I found out this weekend. I've been itching for hitching. Hitchhiking—getting out on the road, getting footloose. Just winging it. Flying by the seat of my pants.

The Army provides me with a very structured life; I do what I'm told and I try my best to work hard. I've lived strictly as a model soldier, quiet, trustworthy, respectful and easy to get along with. But that life is quickly getting old; in fact, it's been in the hospital for some time now, with tubes and various instruments hopelessly struggling to keep the wheezing and emaciated life from dying of consumption, to prolong the life just a little bit longer. The doctors gravely inform me that the death of that life will come by June, when my four year enlistment is up and I become a civilian again.

So what happens when that life finally croaks? I'll be free, that's what. And when I get out I intend to enjoy my freedom to the fullest extent. I've got my passport, but the most important asset I've acquired for my Great Adventure is gumption—the willingness to go for it, even if you don't know exactly what it is. Gumption provides the momentum, the driving force, and the courage.

I think to myself, "Ok, so you want to live this adventurous and happy-go-lucky lifestyle, but you don't know anything about it! You've never done it and you don't even know if you'll like it. You really need to get out there in the world and have a little mini adventure to see if that's the kind of life you really want to live in the future." I accept the logic that major life decisions should be made after thorough research and evaluation. The decision for me to become a vagabond when

I leave the Army is a serious choice, and I'd like to follow it through. Well…maybe it's not that serious.

So anyway, this Labor Day came around and I had nothing to do. Not a thing in the world to do for four days. Not a plan in my head. I reckoned it was time to go for it, to go hitchhiking, and get out in the world. I informed my close friend, Darquist Williams, and he said simply, "Well, good luck", not believing that I would ever get picked up, imagining I'd return in a couple hours, defeated and bored again. Fortunately, things didn't turn out quite that way.

Friday

Friday morning, my alarm clock wails, and the first excited little thought of the morning whispers to me, "Today's the day. Grab your stuff. Today we're going for it!" Sleepily, I pilot my junky, but faithful, old car out to a lonesome gas station on a highway, grab my gear and a road map of North Carolina, and stand out on the road with my thumb in the air towards the traffic and an idiot grin on my face. That's where my story of this weekend really begins. I intend to keep this narrative as true to life as I can, and I'm telling you right now you may not believe that crazy stuff like this really does happen.

Now, I wait. Awww, oh God help me! Is anybody ever going to pick me up? Was my friend Williams right? Is this whole endeavor just a foolish waste of time? Nobody stops for hitchhikers anymore. America is a place where you just don't do that. Everyone who passes looks at me like I'm delusional. I don't like standing in front of people like this. What are they all thinking and saying about me? But, oh well, I'll just wait, at least a little longer. I'll just stand here like a statue and maybe learn a thing or two about patience. I stretch and tire my face from forcing myself to show my teeth in an effort to appear harmless. This first attempt at a prolonged carnival grin feels unnatural and unpleasant.

A car slows down and pulls over. The smiling driver points at me and beckons me in. I'm saved! It works! People do care; they will help each other! This is the first ride of my entire life, and I'm as excited as an astronaut in an arboretum. It's a completely unique moment: an entry from the square Army life, with the endless rules, schedules, and regulations, into the complete opposite: a rotund Bohemian life, chock full of chance and adventure.

I run to the car, carrying everything I own for the weekend. I'm laden with a medium sized backpack, packed with a light fleece top and bottom, a tarp, spare drawers (for if I crap my pants), water bottles, various snacks, and my gumption (of course). Shorts and a t-shirt loosely gird my skinny body, and Jesus sandals protect my five-toed road stompers. This ought to be enough equipment to get me by just fine for the four days. I was wrong; it was too much! With this lifestyle, simpler equals better. Things come and they go, just as natural as you let them. The necessities are easy to find, especially in the overabundance that is America.

So I meet the driver, John, a highly paid, abundantly educated professional driving a brand new car. And what a first-rate trip it was! I couldn't ask for anything better. John was as enthused to pick me up as I was to get picked up.

John says, "So where are you headed?"

I hesitate, furrowing my brows, "West, towards the mountains."

John says, "Well, I'm only going about 15 miles up the road, but I'll gladly take you up to the next exit."

I say, "Cool, man I really appreciate it!"

John says, "You don't have any particular destination in mind?"

I say, "No I just stuck out my thumb and sort of...you know, went for it. Just to see where I end up.

John says, "Wow! You're a man after my own spirit!"

I say, "Oh yeah?"

John says, "Yeah I used to do the same thing, just have

adventures and roam around. I remember sleeping in caves in Crete."

I say, "Sweet, that's what it's about, having adventures. We might as well enjoy our freedom while we've got it."

John says, "I can't believe it. I really admire you. You're just the way I was when I was young. Of course now I'm married with a kid, but I still like to get out and try those old adventurin' ways now and again."

I say, "Sweet. Party on, dude."

John says, "And I love to see someone just getting out and experiencing the world like that. You don't see it much nowadays, especially around here. I guess that's the reason I picked you up.

We ramble on excitedly in the same vein until he drops me off and heads to work. He writes his phone number on a scrap of paper and says he'll buy me a beer when I come back to Fayetteville, and he'd love to hear how it all ends up.

After John, I catch my next ride down the highway with a general laborer from El Salvador in his work truck. I had the greatest success rate hitching with Latinos and the lowest rate with the Blacks. The Whites fell somewhere in the middle. Other minorities are negligible in this part of the country. I'm white myself. From this, I conclude that Latinos kick ass; you can interpret my meticulous research as you like.

People who looked poor, or as if they had been down on their luck a time or two, were much more likely to give me rides. Most good Samaritans who picked me up had hitchhiked at one point in their lives, so they knew how hard it can be, standing on the side of the road, watching empty cars pass. Hitchhiking has no fixed rules for who will pick you up and who won't. Every time I believed that I had the whole thing down to a science, someone who I wouldn't expect at all would pick me up and blow away all my prejudices and stereotypes. All you can do (if you're smart and willing) is stick your thumb out and smile at everyone.

Walking through a slow town, I stop at a roadside fruit stand and converse with the proprietor, an inbred-looking sort of older fellow with most of his teeth missing and a pair of squinty eyes hidden way back in the fat of his head. We chat slowly, like two lazy Southern possums; he was a very pleasant guy, despite his appearance. He identifies with me, having done a bit of hitchhiking in his youth. He sold me a pair of monstrous peaches for a dollar. I can say, without reservation, that they were the very best peaches I've devoured in my entire life. With zest, I stuff my empty stomach. Victuals taste so much better like this, when you just happen upon them randomly, like a hunter-gatherer.

Another work van takes me to Raleigh, where a contractor picks me up as soon as I find a spot to hitch. He says, "You hungry? Where do you want to go for lunch? I'll take you anywhere man, my treat. We got a Schlotzky's deli right over there, that place is *The Bomb*." He emphasizes "The Bomb" theatrically, like a radio advertiser. I accept his munificent offer and wonderingly demolish a delicious toasted sandwich, pastrami on wheat. The guy drives me out of his way to a good hitching spot and offers me some cash for the road. I decline the cash, telling him to save it for somebody who actually needs it. I end up giving the rest of my combo meal away to a bum on the side of the road. This raggedy old bum tells me about 'being saved', and then his cell phone rings. Bums with cellular telephones, do wonders never cease out here?

A soldier from Fort Bragg picks me up. He's a brand new private in the Army, and he tells me all sorts of crazy stories, wildly embellishing them in an attempt to impress me by his vast life experience. Of course, I only know that he's lying because I'm also a soldier, and I've been in a few years myself.

But I don't tell him about that; instead, I just act amazed and ask typical civilian questions. He drops me off at a truck stop.

The truck stop is *The Spot* to be for serious hitchhiking, and a big tractor trailer is *The Ride* to catch. Sometimes you have to wait a little longer for a truck, but that initial investment of time pays off exponentially. If I was trying to travel home to California, I wouldn't hitch anything but semis. The truckers will take care of you, and they're often glad to have some company to alleviate the lonely hours of their monotonous job.

As soon as I stick out my thumb a semi pulls over and I run towards it gleefully. An enormous middle-aged Hispanic trucker sits on the driver's seat. An enormous, ancient cowboy hat rests on the head of the enormous Latino trucker. He wears his button-up shirt wide open, revealing tattoos and various scars on his torso from only God know what. The inside of his arms bear old marks around the joint, tracks from shooting heroin. His belly reaches toward the steering wheel like a hairy brown watermelon, hungry for power and control of the truck, but restrained by his pants, which don't appear to be zipped up or buttoned at all. His pants and belly are stalemated in a war against each other, a war that has been going on for a long time and will continue to go on for a long time.

I jump in. He grins. I grin.

His smile is good natured, proud, and honest. We keep each other company with some of the greatest conversation that I've had since I sat with my buddies in a guard tower in Afghanistan. Sometimes, I actually used to look forward to guard duty; it was the perfect time to get everything off of your chest, and connect with someone on a deep level. Circumstances like that—stuck together in a small space for a prolonged period of time can breed some of the best conversation ever, but it can be miserable too.

He chain smokes Marlboro Reds, and we talk about everything. We talk about hitching, life, his hacienda, family, traveling, drugs, money, happiness, hookers (known as lot lizards by truckers), crime, history, religion, and God. His name is Eriberto. People call him Herbie. Below is an excerpt from one of his speeches. All the colorful expletives have been censored by me. If you like, you can imagine them, just stick a drawled out ***** between every second or third word.

Man I just don't like no preacher telling me how to live my life, you know what I mean? All they want is power, all they want is to tell you what to do. They don't know God. I want to know God. You don't know God from doing what that preacher man tell you to do. Me, I want a personal relationship with Jesus. That's something that some other person can't give you. Sure I sometimes mess up. Sometimes I do wrong. Ok, a lot of time I do wrong. But I try, you know? Sometimes I slip up. Like being out here on the road it's hard. That's why I make sure I'm home every single week. Your wife, sometimes she needs the meat, you know what I'm saying? And if you ain't there then it's going to be someone else. You like black women? I like black women. Cost me a lot of money, man, bad habits. I slept with two female truckers. I feel bad man, I've got this sin weighing on my heart, and this sin, it kills the spirit. That's what sin does.

Herbie and I transition from topic to topic with ease. We speak extensively about racism, and it's now more confusing to me than it ever was. He sees the world in terms of colors. He says the most bigoted things and then follows that statement with something straight from his kind heart. He was, undeniably, a great hypocrite, simultaneously an unmerciful tyrant and a benevolent humanitarian. An intense streak of both the good and the bad gushed through him.

Introducing him, I characterized him as a Hispanic. That's what he looks like. But throughout the course of our graphic and thoughtful conversation he showed me that even though people look a certain way, once you get to know them they're really just other people. I can't adequately express the profound impression he made on me. Like the endless struggle between his belly and his pants, he fights a continual battle between the good and the bad, inside himself, all of the time.

Herbie would have taken me all the way to the Mexican border with him, and I would've gone in a heart beat, if it hadn't been for the fact that I have to be back in the unforgiving ranks by Tuesday at 0600. He and I really hit it off good. Instead, practical considerations dictated that I halt in the foothills of the Appalachian Mountains. After a final handshake, I lurch off the truck and stagger from the interstate into a cluster of road building equipment, where I hose down the nearest tractor with a deluge of urine. Oh Lord, I was absolutely dying. I had been holding it for a solid hour, and that Gatorade I drank threatened to burst my bladder with every bump we bobbed over. But it felt orgasmic to let it all go. That's the road for you: continual extremes of pleasure and pain.

I catch a couple of rides and keep heading west. A jolly paramedic abandons me at a deserted intersection way out in the boondocks. Grey hooligan rain clouds hover ominously close, jeering at me because of my vulnerable condition. They just can't wait to douse me so that I'll never get a ride. Who's going to stop in a God forsaken forest to pick up a tall, strange hitchhiker in the dark rain? That exact scene can be found in a baker's dozen of horror flicks. I do not want to spend the night here. Just as the cantankerous grey puffs swell up and begin throwing their first drops of liquid cloud vomit all over the earth, a diminutive, middle-aged single woman picks me up. She's a Christian, straight out of the Bible thumping Belt. She saw me standing on the onramp, so she took the next exit and looped back around, all merely to help me out. The weather commences beating the windshield, but soon gives up, realizing that I've outfoxed it for the time being. Sweet Triumph! Score: Clark 1, Weather 0!

The Christian lady said that it was God's will that she was coming by at that moment to pick me up. I'm all smiles—

23

finally, a woman with some honest, strong faith who will practice what she believes in! Finally, I meet a Christian who will act like a Christian, and help out somebody who needs help. Because when I'm out on the road I need help. I live and travel by other's kindness and mercy. It's a form of living off of faith in something that you can't see, and it feels fantastic.

Next, a very redneck couple picks me up. They drive a trashed, mid 1980's vintage, full size Chevrolet van, with pastel pink interior and captain's chairs all around. The man sports the gnarliest mullet I've ever seen, and the woman in her dingy sweatpants could certainly win a frumpy pageant. But at least she shows some taste; she's rocking some sweet Led Zeppelin flip flops. I compliment her on them. They're on their way to an Indian casino in the mountains, just past Asheville. The man offers me a cold beer. They're driving with an ice chest full of Bud Light. I immediately and gratefully accept the proffered beverage. Contentedly, I sip on my icy cold Bud and reflect on how the rides just keep getting better; I watch the misty mountains drift by. We all talk slowly and without any pressure. They say "Cool, Man", in reply to most of my answers. These mellow folks live life at a slow pace, and I share their world for an hour or two. They're remarkable only for their hillbilliness. Friendly, open, unpretentious, and generous, these are the best kind of people to meet and to spend time with.

The sun yawns, blinks sleepily, and checks the clock for the time. It's nearly time for Mr. Sun to go home for the evening. I ask the couple to drop me off in Asheville. They drive several miles out of their way to put me downtown. I thank them profusely.

A mountain sports store lures me in. The cashier is a young college student named Joe, conservatively dressed and respectable looking. Joe says, "Can I help you?"

I say, "Maybe you can. Here's the deal. I just hitchhiked in from Fayetteville. I really didn't have much of a plan and now I'm here. Perhaps you know of a cheap local hostel where I could crash tonight?"

Joe says, "Wow, that's crazy man. They dropped you off right here?"

I say, "Yeah, my last ride just drove off. Real nice couple of rednecks. Comfortable van, gave me a cold beer. It was solid."

Joe, laughing, says, "Wow, that's pretty adventurous. I actually don't know of any local hostels, but I'll look on the internet right here and see if I can find something out for you."

I say, "Cool, thanks dude, I really appreciate it."

Joe says, "So, you have no plans tonight?"

I say, "Hmmm... This weekend is happening entirely without plans. Yes, there will be no plans whatsoever. I just totally wing it and see what happens. Is anything cool happening here tonight?"

Joe says, "There's a concert with The Thumbs playing, that's where my friend and I will probably go."

I say, "Huh, never heard of them. What else is there to do?"

Joe says, "Let's see, not too much. This town is pretty dull. Whatever you do, stay away from Prichard Park."

I say, "Why, what's Prichard Park?"

Another employee chimes in, "Oh yeah, stay away from Prichard Park. It's crazy over there."

Joe says, "Yeah, there's a bunch of hippies and trustafarians that hang out at this park on Friday night. They have some sort of big drum circle. Everyone gets in a pit and dances. It's really crazy, actually I'd try to stay away from downtown Asheville if I were you."

I say, "That doesn't sound so bad. It actually sounds like a lot of fun."

The other employee says, "No it's bad, man, too weird. Bunch of loonies. Packed with people."

I say, "Ok, show me where this park is, so I don't accidentally go there."

The employees take out a city map and circle the park. Of course, they piqued my curiosity with the first mention of the park, and now I'm dying to go check it out. What kind of hippie scene could they have in Asheville, North Carolina? I presumed that it wasn't much, maybe just a couple poseurs. Never in my life have I been more mistaken.

I hoof it down Tunnel Road, towards the park. A few girls in cars yowl out catcalls to me, and a few teenage boys scream unintelligible curses. The teenage boys are, by far, the worst group I encountered on the road. Two or three times over the course of the four day weekend I was yelled at and flipped off, all by teenage boys.

As I approach Tunnel Road's namesake, the light escaping from the long tunnel shines strangely, projecting a garish and surreal image. It shimmers like the portal to some bizarre and otherworldly place. Walking through it, the sound from the cars stretches out dreamlike in my ears, and I am in limbo, in a dirty white tube of nothingness, like a larva in a cocoon, pupating into a butterfly.

Emerging from the tunnel, I spot a young couple up on a

high patio in a business district, jamming on the violin and guitar. I smile and stop. I walk on. I stop again, and think. I have a modest choice to make here. I could walk on and mind my own business. Or I could go up and listen to them jam, which may open up a whole realm of new possibilities. Two things I know for sure: I've got nothing to lose by going up there to check out the scene, and I'll never know what could have happened if I don't. Musicians are generally a free thinking and liberal bunch, and I'm sure they wouldn't mind a small audience. I decide to go for the gusto. I will seize the day, even if all that means is going up and meeting strangers on the street.

I make my way up the steep incline, and circle around the back to the patio. A gaggle of eccentric young men loiter around the entrance to a building prominently marked 'Studio'. I walk past them and introduce myself to the talented musicians, Michelle and Ryan, who are friendly and chilled out. They jam, freestyling with the guitar and the violin. I inquire as to their plans for the evening, and what they can recommend for entertainment. They're going to be here for a couple of hours; they're preparing to film for a local television show. Michelle says we should exchange phone numbers; maybe we could hang out later.

Troy, the host of the television show called 'The Anti-Show', comes out and meets me. The story of my day impresses him, so he invites me into the studio to hang out and see the band that's about to start playing. I sit by myself in the filming area, a couple feet away from the lead singer, who sports dreadlocks down to his thighs! The band absolutely rocks. I've never heard such good tunes. I applaud enthusiastically every time they finish a song. The video footage probably looks a little strange, with these charismatic Rastafarians jamming away, and a single grinning idiot clapping in the background. Next, a metal band shows up, and their cacophony of ugly sounds drives me away from the studio.

Again, I find myself drawn magnetically toward Prichard Park. This trek into the depths of downtown Asheville reminds me of the old Vietnam movie, *Apocalypse Now*, or Conrad's book, Heart of Darkness, where the main character probes deeper and deeper into the physical and metaphorical jungle, encountering increasingly bizarre people and situations. It's about nine o'clock in the evening, and the whole town is bustling. It becomes progressively weirder; then I hear the distant sound of a rhythm.

As I draw near, the primal beat thumps first through the air, then on my skin, then on into my muscles, and finally into my bones, until my whole body tingles with hippie electricity. At last, I round a corner and see the crowd standing at the edge of a pit. Freaks were everywhere: cults, hippies, gypsies, college students, rockers, punks, bums, artists, musicians, and a few straight up wing nuts. A couple of monkish, bearded young men dressed in homespun brown tunics catch my eye; they hold a sign that reads, "Does wealth correlate with happiness?" I regret passing them by without speaking to them.

Prichard Park is set up like an amphitheater, with stadium style seating. It's the perfect size to host this type of gathering. Probably close to 1,000 people loiter in the general vicinity. On one edge, about thirty musicians thump out a completely unstructured rhythm on various types of drums. The music soars and leaps, jumps and charges, creeps and speeds, all on its own random spontaneity. Nobody controls it. In the crowded bottom of the pit a couple hundred people writhe and dance in tune with the jungle beat. Probably 90 percent of them are crunchy young hippie chicks. I desperately want to get down in the pit and get down. I feel like a spectator to some primitive tribe of aboriginals, or like a witness to some pulsating pagan beat festival/ritual.

I look for the hostel supposedly located downtown so that I can drop my bag and join in on the dancing. I can't find it. Everyone I speak to tells me to go in the opposite direction. Nobody has even heard of the hostel. At an internet café I look it up and discover that it costs fifty dollars a night. Forget that! I must have misheard Joe, the employee at the mountain store, say fifteen. For that kind of money I'd rather sleep in the bushes. I give up on the hostel idea and patronize the first bar I find. I sorely need a refreshing beverage.

This bar is just setting up the equipment for a live techno show, so I drink some of the delicious and reasonably priced local organic beer while making small talk with the owner of the place, a very groovy young woman from San Francisco.

Small schools of coy college babes swim around the streets like fish. This is a big change for me from the typical male infested Army base. I pull myself together and saunter on back to the television studio to watch the musicians jam.

Inside the actual editing studio, I am impressed with all the high tech and professional gadgetry these crazy folks have access to. Michelle, the violinist, is about to do a solo. She can't see me behind the dark glass. She plays and sings for the camera. Oh Lord, she is beautiful, and so talented! I love the way she just stands there awkwardly, stock still, arms at her sides, not moving a muscle, but exquisitely singing her heart out. Her obvious honesty appeals to me in a big way. She's not a cardboard cutout from television singing some more popular trash, but an authentic individual, with sincere music. Usually people are too scared to get out there, to do what they love, and to expose their innermost treasures and talents so vulnerably to the world like that; she does, and I admire her for it.

Michelle sings her last set and comes into the lobby. We talk and hit it off, so she drives me out in her Lexus SUV to a vegan restaurant for dinner. The place is packed. We meet one of the handsome dreadlocked members of the first band to play at the studio. He tells us about the mystical power of crystals, and invites us to some sort of gathering which happens according to the ancient Mayan lunar calendar. I would have gone if I had the time, but, lamentably, my strict military schedule doesn't jive with the Mayan lunar calendar. One would think that my superiors could have paid more attention to that when planning training and deployments. I ask the musically adept space cadet if I can touch his dreadlocks, as that is the hairstyle that I aspire for when I'm legally permitted to grow my hair out more than an inch. Smiling, the space cadet says, "Yeah man, feel away." My sense of adventure, once again, overcomes my sense of propriety, and I fondle his dreads. They feel like some kind of natural rope, and they're lighter than I expected. He uses one strand to tie up all the others and form a ponytail. I totally dig it.

I order some silly vegan dish I've never heard of before, and some more homegrown organic beer to wash it down. The thought rambles through my mind, "what could I possibly be chewing on right now?" Oh well, who cares. It tastes quite scrumptious, whatever it is.

Michelle says, "So what are your plans for tonight?"

I say, "I'm hanging out with you right now, and beyond that I'm not so sure."

Michelle says, "I mean, where are you going to stay tonight?"

I say, "I was going to stay at this hostel, but I couldn't find it, and it was too expensive anyway. So I'll probably just sleep under some bushes somewhere."

Michelle says, "You've got to be kidding me."

I say, "I'm dead serious. It won't bother me too much, just so long as it doesn't rain."

Michelle, laughing, says, "No way, that's crazy."

I say, "Maybe just a little unconventional. Have you heard of Couchsurfing?"

Michelle says, "Yeah I think I have, it's a website right?"

I say, "Yeah, it's a website where people who enjoy meeting characters from all over the world offer their homes to other people. It's a cultural exchange thing, kind of like having a foreign exchange student, but only for a couple of days. I was going to get online and find someone, but I don't have the internet where I live, and this whole trip was really completely unplanned. I'm just flying by the seat of my pants."

Michelle says, "Wow that's really cool, sounds like fun. Well, I really wish I could offer you to stay at my house, but I'm sleeping in the guest bedroom because there's a bunch of stuff in my room, from when I moved."

I smirk and slyly say, "Perhaps you have a couch?"

Michelle says excitedly, "Oh yeah! That would be cool, my parents wouldn't care! You can come home with me and have a place to stay! You won't have to sleep in the bushes! Yay!"

I say, "Totally sweet! I really appreciate it. If it wasn't for people helping other people then nobody would get anywhere."

So Michelle takes me home to her folks. The roads twist and turn sinuously through the curves of the affable green mountains. Michelle assures me that she's not just going to take me out somewhere in the middle of nowhere and kill me. I laugh. About midnight, we arrive at her beautiful castle way up in the mountains. Everything about it is phenomenal, really top of the line. As if I couldn't tell by the Lexus, her family is very well off. The view out of the back porch takes my breath away; you can look out from the top of the mountain and see the lights in the valleys below. The mountains are sometimes the same color as the sky, so the lights on the hill appear to be lights in a skyscraper. But these skyscrapers are all natural dirt.

The grand tour of the home winds up outside, by the heated pool, where I remark, "You know, I haven't been swimming for a long time."

Michelle says, "Oh yeah?"

I say, "Yeah, and it's a shame, I would really love a swim right now. Actually that sounds like a great idea." I remove all clothing, except my underwear, and dive straight into the deep end."

Michelle laughs and says, "Oh my goodness, you are crazy!"

I come up shivering and say, "WOOOWEEEE! That was a little bit chillier than I'd first expected."

Michelle steps out of her clothes, but retains her underwear for modesty's sake. "Okay mister, if you're going to do it, I'm going to do it."

I say, "All right, that's the spirit! Now jump in!" Michelle enters the water slowly, by the steps, refusing to go past her belly button. Suddenly, I hear the sound of a door closing and an unfamiliar voice.

The voice yells out worryingly, "Michelle?!"

Michelle says, "Yeah Mom!"

The voice says, "Where are you?!"

Michelle says, "We're down in the pool!"

The voice says, "Who is we?!"

Michelle says, "My friend and I!"

The voice says, "Ok I'm coming down there!"

Michelle whispers to me, "Oh shoot, it's my Mom! What should we do?!"

I whisper back, "It will be all right." At this point, I don't know what to think or do. My mind blanks completely, leaving me once again a smiling idiot who does crazy things. I've certainly gotten myself into an awkward situation. Here's the facts: This woman, Michelle's mother, is coming onto the scene at about one o'clock in the morning to find her twenty year old daughter nearly nude in the pool, with an equally disrobed strange man, a hitchhiker, who her daughter just happened to randomly pick up downtown and invite home, out of the generosity of her heart. I think about lying, about making up some story about how I'm one of Michelle's college friends, and we've known each other for a long time, and so on and so on. But I don't. I just do what I always do, and let it all hang out. I play it cool and stay honest. You can't go wrong with the truth.

Betty, Michelle's Mom, enters wearing a long pajama top. Michelle greets her with an innocent, "Hey Mom!"

Betty says, "Hi honey, who's this?"

Michelle says, "This is Clark. Clark this is my Mom, Betty." I wave and grin, thinking a handshake might be a little inappropriate, given the circumstances.

I say, "Nice to meet you."

In a friendly tone of voice, Betty says, "Yeah, so, um, who are you?"

I say, "I'm a soldier out of Fort Bragg, right near Fayetteville."

Betty says, "How did you two meet?"

I say, "Well I was walking down the road when I saw Michelle up on a hill playing her violin. I thought I ought to go talk to her, so I did. I watched her record for the television show. She's awesome, you've got quite a daughter. Now I find myself here."

Betty asks, "Why were you just walking down the road?"

I say, "Because I hitchhiked into town."

Betty says, "Oh really? Wow, that's pretty uncommon. And where were you planning on staying tonight?"

I say, "Anywhere I could. Probably under some bushes. But your daughter invited me home. She said you all had a spare couch. That sounded a lot better than the bushes for me."

Michelle says, "Yeah, Mom is it cool if Clark stays the night?"

Betty says, "That will be fine, I just want you two sleeping in separate rooms. So, Clark, what made you want to come to Asheville?"

I say, "I didn't especially want to come to Asheville. I just stuck out my thumb and ended up here. I don't really have a plan. I just had to get out of the barracks this weekend and thought it would be a perfect time to try a little hitchhiking trip, you know, to see whether it works or not. It works great!"

I'd like to say that my candor disarmed both Michelle and Betty, but I really can't take any credit for their generosity, trustfulness, and good nature. In our society, trusting someone, especially a stranger (*gasp!*) is considered reckless and dangerous.

Michelle moves the stuff out of her spare room, so I can sleep in a real bed. I shower, change into my fleece pajamas, and fall asleep chuckling at this marvelously fortunate day.

Saturday

In the middle of the night I wake up to use the bathroom. By the sink I find a large bag of prescription drugs. Curious, I pull out the first bottle. Lithium. Prescribed to Michelle. Oh man. This little discovery dampens my spirits. The idea of antidepressants depresses me immensely, and Lithium is reputed to be one of the gnarliest on the market. I put the bottle back, and try not to guess what all the rest of her many medications could be. I'm not disappointed by Michelle, but rather by the conditions of the world which make so many beautiful, rich people turn to mind-altering substances to get through life. Why? I don't know.

The next morning I awake slowly and pleasantly; this indulgence is such a change from my normal blaring alarm clock offending my ears at obscene hours on the weekday. I lazily drift in and out of dreamland until Michelle comes in to check on me.

We make breakfast: scrambled eggs, fresh fruit and bacon. Deeelicious! The bacon we leave unattended on the burner while we devour our cooked yellow chicken fetuses, until we notice a steady stream of smoke rising from the stove. I hustle to the scene, ascertaining that the bacon has been transformed into an unrecognizable black mass of grease and ashes. That stove was much more potent than I had supposed. I jettison the cremated pig pieces into the outside trash can. The smoke detectors in the house begin to wail, and continue for 15 minutes. Even this fire alarm doesn't wake up Michelle's brother Ryan, a senior in high school. He sleeps like the dead.

The rest of the morning we spend puttering around the house, relaxing and taking it easy, quite possibly my favorite pastime. My original plan had been to hitchhike out that morning so that I could make it back to my place of duty before I was considered AWOL, but everything was going so nicely that I procrastinated and decided Sunday would be fine for hitching back. I ask Michelle if this arrangement will be fine by her; she gladly acquiesces and that is that.

Betty and Daniel, Michelle's mother and stepfather, arrive

home from the market in town after our incident with the bacon. Betty presents us with some appetizing, freshly baked pastries. Then she cooks some more bacon and I chomp that too. I'm a bottomless pit, but Betty's slew of hearty victuals satiates my ravenous belly. I apologize for the awkward circumstances of the previous night, and we all converse pleasantly in the living room. Betty is the perfect Mom, and I love her for it. We talk about all sorts of topics; she's very interested in my life and my circumstances. I'm flattered to be the object of such compassionate and loving care and interest. In no time at all I'm assimilated into the family and made to feel as welcome as can be, like an old friend. Daniel, a retired banker, is also very hospitable. They share their home and their lives with me.

Michelle takes me to the local apple festival in the nearby town of Hendersonville. We eat the best crunchy apples in the world, an experimental type not yet available on the market. Throngs of people pack the street solid for at least five blocks. We meander through the crowd, the booths, and the downtown shops, enjoying the hometown atmosphere and delicious apple smoothies. Several clean cut young men bedecked in sunglasses, white shirts with ties, and black slacks hold up signs that literally read, "God says that gay people will burn in hell!" and various other messages of that nature. It strikes me as a bit odd that these devotees to Christianity, a religion of love, are out here making fools of themselves by aggressively preaching a message of hate and intolerance.

I want to see Asheville in the daytime, so off we go. We wander randomly through the avenues. The local artists and musicians of Asheville remind me of a ragtag horde of wacky relatives, and in the course of a couple hours, Michelle meets at least thirty old friends on the street, which is the living room for the family of off-beat people in Asheville. Two of her friends, a pair of lesbian stage actors, are erotically kissing outside of a theater. We stop and I'm introduced. I find myself alarmingly attracted to the one with hairy legs and armpits. But, hey, besides that she's a total fox, what with her beautiful curly hair, perfect teeth, and olive skin. She just has the kind of manner that totally makes me comfortable. I laugh at myself for my strange caprices. Michelle and I ramble on.

We enter a tattoo shop, and I teeter on the brink of depositing the first permanent ink on my body. I think better of it, and we move on. Outside of the shop we discover Troy, the tv host from last night, talking to the same two bearded, monk-looking men that I saw holding the sign at the drum circle last night. I introduce myself and sit down beside them. They smell like monks, as if they wear the same clothes every day and their bodies haven't been washed in years. That smell conjures up strong associations for me, and I like it. Their names are Maciah and Glen. Maciah relates his story to me.

I used to run a fashionable clothing company in New York. I was very popular, living the life of fame, fashion, glamour, and money. But it was all empty for me. I met a fellow who made me question it all, and I decided to give everything up. I literally threw my expensive stereo and all my worldly goods off a bridge and into the river. (He chuckles fondly at the memory.) It felt fantastic! Since then I've been trying to live the life of a first century Christian. It's been about nine years now. We study the Bible, and diligently and thoroughly apply the instructions to ourselves, which is a task that most people who call themselves Christians are not willing to undertake. They won't carry out their duty as a disciple of Christ to the full and glorious extent. All my brothers and I share everything that we have, and we don't work conventional jobs for the things of this world. Think about how God provides everything for the birds of the air and beasts of the land. If he does all this for mere creatures, then imagine how much he will do for a man, made in his image, who he loves! It's no use worrying about tomorrow, because God will always see us through. I've never regretted my decision one bit. God provides over and above everything that we could ever need. People are so generous; they'll give us houses to stay in and food to eat. Thrift stores throw clothes away because they just get too many. We wear the extra clothes. America consumes an incredible amount of utterly superfluous material goods. So many people go through their lives without thinking. They don't question their basic values. Look where they spend their time. At least forty hours per week are spent serving the almighty dollar. They work for the money so they can buy things that they think they need. We have rejected all that, and we encourage others to reject it also.

Maciah's sermon hits me deep. I know exactly what he's talking about. It's the same thing as hitchhiking. Instead of living on some false certainty and security, you live on faith. This faith, this letting go, is freedom. Maciah is much wealthier than any of the retired old tourists running around with money burning holes in their pockets, because his wealth comes from a healthy spirit, which is the only kind of wealth that never requires antidepressants.

I look at walking around downtown Asheville in two ways. The first way, which the vast majority of folks participate in, is the square way. The Squares yearn for less valuable things, the external objects and appearances. They shop to buy what pleases them. Above all, they are material consumers. They grit their teeth and spend entire lives working jobs that they would rather not, to enable them to have money. Security, regulations, schedules, and budgets are sacred words for them. They like things in packages. They like their experiences neatly boxed up and predictable. They always abide by rules, and fret if they suppose they might be in violation of a minor statute. They go on guided tours. They enjoy sleeping in a motel room that looks identical to a million other motel rooms in this country. Every manner of commercial advertising is directed towards this type of unreflective person, and it's great for a capitalist economy when they just keep on spending that ever flowing money. One more thing—they never pick up hitchhikers.

The second way is the adventurous way. These people live for the internal things, things not bought or sold. They pick up and treasure human experiences, which can't be lost or stolen. These experiences are feather light, and can be carried everywhere, like Santa Claus' magic sleigh full of presents. They appreciate the arts in a very special way—music, theater, art, and literature. Their most cherished possession might be a torn and dirty paperback novel, or a scratched copy of a compact disc. They enjoy leisure and unhurried, insightful conversation. Most importantly, they are known to frequently pick up a friendly hitchhiker.

Obviously, I'm trying to behave the adventurous way this weekend. My polarization of these two modes of living is far too polemical; I know. Everyone has a trace of both inside of them, just like good and evil. But we should all try to at least be conscious of what we are and how we live.

Nudging me, Michelle silently mouths, "let's go". I take the hint and shake Maciah's hand, bidding him goodbye. Michelle reaches forth to do the same, but he pulls his hand back quickly, as if her touch would burn him like a branding iron. Michelle is offended and asks me later why he behaved like that; I explain that he completely abstains not only from any kind of sexual act, but also from all physical contact with women. Sounds like a pretty sound policy to me. I'm quiet, mulling over Maciah's way of life. If I wasn't in the Army, I would leave Michelle right then and there and join him and his group. They give up everything in order to gain a little something worth having, that pearl of great price. Their Christianity and their faith is totally honest, and far beyond the norm in America today. I like the idea of religion being all or nothing. I know it would be interesting to live that extreme way of life with them, even if just for a little while.

We saunter on, and enter the Dripolator, a funky coffee house. The seating is made of some strange material bent in unconventional but comfortable shapes. Couches and tables crowd the place; I'd say this little joint could hold nearly a hundred people, with ease. I totally dig these coffee places. Young people and students sprawl everywhere, reading, writing, studying, and talking. These laid back lounges are the forums of the town, places to do more than just drink coffee;

here you can meet and interact with people. Michelle knows the employee on duty; she and he are both manic-depressive. She asks him general questions about his life, and he answers in equally general terms. I ask him whether he's hitchhiked before, as he looks like he might be that kind of guy. He says that he spent a full year in Europe hitchhiking, and that it's much easier on the other side of the Atlantic. In Europe it's a more culturally accepted endeavor, and thus more people do it, and thus more people are willing to pick people up. This is all I need to hear. If I wasn't in the Army, I'd hitchhike to the airport, buy a ticket and fly to Europe that day. Unfortunately, I'll have to postpone my impulsive plans until the summer.

Along the streets, we encounter many musicians busking for change. Michelle knows all of them, without exception. The talent of the street performers exceedingly impresses me, but, then again, I'm not accustomed to hearing quality live music.

Michelle decides she wants to take me dancing in South Carolina. I say, "Right on, I'm there." We hop in the car, and off we go. The excursion through these mountains at twilight presents me with the most picturesque view of the Appalachians anyone could ask for. Acres of lush lawns with antique homes, farms, and barns periodically break through the friendly forest. For me, this is America. This rural vision I will always revere in my heart. I stare wide eyed out the window like a small child, enthralled with the world.

A very portly old barn peeks out from behind a bend in the road. As we drive up, it seems to smile and invite us to go dancing. Behind the barn, a lazy little creek flows sleepily, while a man bathes in it. The atmosphere is perfect and no bugs are in sight. This place feels like paradise to me. A couple of smiling hippies wave to us from the patio. Michelle pays our admission and we enter. Inside, the dance hall charms just like the outside. Christmas tree lights illuminate the entire establishment with a suffused, cozy glow. On the back wall, drinks and freshly cut watermelon compete for space on a table. On our right is a stage, where the live band will be performing. Old couches line the entire wall to our left. I sink into one; the cushions cradle me with very comfortable, typical southern hospitality.

The beginner lesson commences. Funky looking old men with white hair don dancing shoes and skirts, so they can get their groove on better. The kilts do look mighty comfortable for rocking out in. I silently curse our prejudiced society, which allows women to wear men's clothes, but won't allow men to wear women's clothes. I wish I was Scottish; then I'd have an excuse. This is a contra dancing hall, and tonight I'll be contra dancing. I wonder to myself, "What in the world is contra dancing?" Michelle, an old hand at contra, is my partner for the lessons. Although I'm the male, and thus supposed to lead the dance, Michelle elegantly guides my bumbling and confused feet through the steps. I enjoy myself immensely, even though I'm facing the wrong way and dancing with myself, half of the time.

People crowd the hall as the beginner lessons end. Beautiful, healthy, smiling, lithe, athletic, rosy-cheeked young babes with solid hips form the majority of the dancers, with a few fruity looking men thrown in for good measure. The women have to dance with each other, because there aren't enough males to go around. I feel like I've been ensnared by a tribe of Amazon women. How could I not enjoy it?

We all dance the dance, twirling, twisting, whirling, rocking, stomping, swinging, smiling, and clapping in perfect time with the beat, except for me. I seem to always be just a tad off. Nevertheless, I grin and have as much fun as a hamster in a hair salon. The pretty girls lead me and show me what to do, and where to go. An extremely lanky, kilted gray haired man flirts with me, smiling and gazing coquettishly into my eyes. I crack up with laughter at the humor of it all. The next dance, I look for a new partner. A legitimate midget holds out her hand to me. I accept it, and off we go. The disparity in our stature forces me to stoop down, but I still love it. You haven't lived until you've danced the contra with a genuine midget.

An hour into it, I'm getting pretty well into the swing of things, having the absolute time of my life, when Michelle informs me she's not feeling quite well, and she'd like to go home. After one more dance, I gracefully yield to her request. She has done so much for me that it doesn't bother me to head home early. I drive the Lexus and reflect on the wild and completely random circumstances, which in the course of a few hours took me from standing dirty and disheveled by the side of the road, with nothing but hope and vague ideas, to driving a beautiful young woman in her luxury SUV to an amiable home, with a family that's practically adopted me. My eyes twinkle, and I laugh to myself. It's like Cinderella all over again.

Back at the house, Michelle's brother Ryan is hosting a sleepover of some five boys, all seniors in high school. Betty lectures Ryan very seriously, threatening punitive action if any of them partake in marijuana or alcohol. She refuses to condone that sort of behavior in her house, and she doesn't want her family burdened by that sort of reputation. Ryan promises with some halfway statements, "Ok Mom, nobody will find out."

"Nobody will find out because you won't be doing it!" Betty retorts shrilly and indignantly.

Betty talks to me, and asks me to watch over them, and kick some ass if things get out of hand. I joke that I'll break out the military hand to hand combat moves, if the need arises. She trusts me, and says that I'm in charge of the house for the night. I'm only 21, and I can hazily recall sleepovers like these as a senior in high school. I feel a lifetime older than these fresh-faced pups. War has put some wrinkles on my forehead. Betty is fighting a fairly hopeless battle against the teenage tendency to misbehave, but at least she fights it.

Michelle and I retire to a blanket on the lawn. We watch the stars, while she reads her poetry and sings her songs to me. Her creations, her art, brings tears to my eyes and touches me way down inside; it's so lovely. We're hopeless romantics, I know.

All my Army buddies will laugh at these admissions, but I don't care. Sometimes we pretend that we're hard, but we're really not.

Sunday

Sunday morning, Michelle rouses me from a very deep sleep. I originally intended to wake at the crack of dawn to get out on the road early, but that didn't happen. I pack my few possessions away, and I'm ready to leave. Walking into the kitchen, I smell Betty's freshly baked cinnamon rolls. Betty is a professional cook, and an incredible one at that. I eat the homemade cinnamon rolls, and speak with Betty and David. Our talk leaves me with the impression that these people really love me and care about me. Words can't express how grateful I am for their hospitality. Betty makes me a sandwich and packs me a nutritious sack lunch for the road. She hugs me warmly, and I'm on my way.

I need to get to the interstate to catch a ride back to the base. As of right now, I have about 40 hours to get back before the four day weekend is over and I'm considered AWOL (absent with out leave). Michelle takes me to the interstate; she's on her way to a fiddle playing gig downtown. The old Lynyrd Skynyrd song repeats itself inside my head, "Lord I was born a ramblin' man / Trying to make a livin' and doin' the best I can / When it's time for leavin', I hope you'll understan' / That I was born a ramblin' man". Michelle feels awkward about just dropping me off on the side of the road. I do my best to reassure her, and thank her for this fairy tale weekend. We part cordially, and again I find myself by the side of the road, with nothing to my name, except for some good memories. That's the way I like it best though. Don't get me wrong; I'd love to settle down in the traditional way, but I know that now is not the appropriate time for that. I intend to enter the domestic family life with no regrets. So many people make commitments before they're ready. I want to know that I made the most of my freedom before I bind myself with obligations.

My good luck on Friday makes me optimistic about my chances of getting back to the base on time. I stand for about an hour before I'm picked up by a woman driving a car completely jammed full of stuff and people. I'm barely able to cram myself in and shut the door. These people are just coming home from church. They offer me more freshly baked cinnamon rolls, which I accept and chew on contentedly. Hallelujah, and Praise the Lord for Southern hospitality!

Throughout the day, I catch an eclectic variety of short rides. Although I'm on the interstate, and I should be moving swiftly, I can't seem to catch a long ride. Hitchhiking is like fishing for people, but it's much more exciting, because instead of catching a mess of identical slimy fish, you catch rides with diverse and genuine people you can connect with, and you have no idea who they're going to be.

A dirty redneck picks me up, rescuing me from the scorching sun. He drinks brown-bagged malt liquor as he drives. He talks to me, but I can't understand even a single word he says; his accent is that thick. Or maybe he's just that drunk. Thankfully, he lets me off at the next exit, which is the absolute middle of nowhere. I have to hoof it a mile or two before I can post myself in my customary place on a freeway onramp. Two cars pass me in an hour. At that rate, I'll be standing here for days before I'm picked up. I go up to the interstate itself and try to hitch. The cars blow by me at 70 miles an hour, and the gusts from the semis nearly bowl me over. I count as more than two hundred of them pass, without even slowing down, and I conclude that it's hopeless.

Assessing my situation, I conclude that it looks quite bleak. According to my road map, today I've traveled 102 miles, and now I'm stranded on the outskirts of Podunkville, NC. It's 154 miles back to the Army barracks. I'm not going to make it back in time. I will be AWOL, and in a whole lot of trouble. I sit down and think. My friend, Chris, went home to Ohio this weekend; therefore, he should be cruising back down this same interstate tomorrow. I call him up on my cellular phone and quickly explain my predicament. He agrees to pick me up tomorrow night on his way through. His promised support relieves me immensely. I can now turn my mind to my more immediate problem—what am I going to do with myself until then?

The somewhat busy onramp, where the redneck picked me up, is about four miles behind me. Looking on my map, I see that the next onramp is at least ten miles ahead, and it looks like it is dead center in the middle of nowhere. My best prospect to escape Podunkville is to walk the four miles back. The sun is about an hour away from setting. I decide to spend the night in the first suitable location I find, and then make the walk in the morning to start hitching early.

I cross the freeway and start walking down this country road at dusk. My fate tonight is in God's hands. Will I have to sleep under a bridge, or in a ditch? I don't know. Beautiful grass and farmland effortlessly covers the countryside; it looks cozy, like fleece pajamas for the earth. This place wouldn't be so bad, if I wasn't stuck here. I consider just walking up to somebody's house and explaining my situation, trying to put myself in some stranger's hands, and maybe they would take care of me, like Michelle and her family did. Musing about this, walking along, I see a glow in the distance. A massive five story hospital is tucked away in the midst of all this nothingness!

I grin at the sight of the hospital. Perhaps my prayers for tonight have been answered. Sleeping in weird and highly unlikely places constitutes an integral part of the whole adventure. Road dust and grit have blackened my bare, sandaled feet, and I'm sweaty and stinky. A shower would be the cat's meow right now. Hospitals are littered with bathrooms and showers for the patients. My smirk turns mischievous, and I approach the hulking, glowing institution of medicine with two simple purposes in mind: washing and sleeping. Perhaps I will become a covert patient here tonight.

Walking tall, I stride into the lobby of the hospital. The

elderly couple volunteering at the desk greets me and asks, "Can I help you?"

Confidently and politely I reply, "No I'm good. Thank you very much." The hallway inside is deserted, so I take the time to study a floor map posted on the wall. Natural logic tells me that the higher floors are more likely to be free of people, especially those pesky cops and security guards.

The elevator brings me to the second floor. A nurse on duty in the lobby glances at me, so I press the 'door close' button and elevate to the third floor. Same deal. I try the fourth floor. Money! Not a soul to be seen! I exit the elevator and examine the signs on the wall. The usually prosaic words 'Sleep Research Center' leap off the sign and fill my heart with gladness. I enter the sleep research center and discover several four inch thick foam mattresses unsecured in the hallway. The doors to the actual labs are locked, but that's fine by me, because with one of those mattresses I'll simply find a little corner somewhere and hide myself away. I notice one particular detail, an hourly log kept by the security guards, posted on the wall. That means this area is patrolled, and I'll have to be careful when I return to borrow the mattress.

Now what about the shower? I continue to explore the

fourth floor, and I discover a wing devoted to exam rooms, the kind that you'd use for any sort of general hospital visits. Each exam room has been magnanimously endowed with its own little bathroom, complete with bathtub, shower, and fresh soap. I lock myself in the bathroom and literally make myself at home. I'm so exulted by my trespassing that I can barely refrain from singing. I indulge in a long and luxurious hot bath. I can't remember the last time I actually took a bath, but it relaxes and does wonders to my weary body as I soak there, reading a book. My entire body wrinkles and turns pink. The combination of sun and sandals has marked my five-toed road stompers with some bizarre tan lines. I scrub away and use an entire bar of hospital soap removing the crud from my feet and lower legs. The water turns gray from the dirt that I wash off. After an hour of this, I take a cool shower, rinsing my sandals and the tub.

This exam room seems as good of a place as any to sleep. I hide my possessions under the counter and steal into the hallway, barefoot, with my wet hair sticking out at all kinds of outlandish angles, looking like a proper vagabond. It's going to be extremely difficult to plausibly excuse myself if I'm caught in the act right now. I left the sandals behind because they squeak on the floor when they're moist. I'm infiltrating the sleep research center, in the process of appropriating a mattress from the gurney where it's stored, when I catch a flash of blue uniformed movement out of my peripheral vision. It's a security guard!

I immediately drop the mattress on the gurney and attempt to hide in a shallow doorway. My heart beats wildly as I clandestinely peek around the corner. He hasn't seen me! Thank God! A windowed set of doors to this wing has blocked his view. He's moving down the hall towards me, trying the doors to see whether they're locked. It will be less than a minute before he stumbles upon me. My mind races feverishly. The one thing I really don't want right now is to be caught. What in the world would I tell my company commander when I call him from the pokey in Podunkville? The only way out of this wing is blocked by the security guard, the seconds are ticking by as he moves towards me, and all the doors are locked, so I'm basically screwed. Maybe I should just walk by him and play it off like this is a completely normal thing? It's either that, or I let him find me obviously hiding. But no conscientious security guard is simply going to let me walk by unquestioned, not in the state that I'm in. I manage to collect myself, cool down, and study my immediate vicinity. A fire escape sign is just down the hall! I'm delivered!

After taking a quick peek for the guard, I slink rapidly down the corridor and into the fire escape staircase. Thankfully, no alarm bells wail, so I run full speed upstairs, past a chain cordoning the uppermost staircase off limits, and I sit by the door to the roof. Time passes, and I regain my composure. He hasn't followed me. It's purely a stroke of luck that he failed to detect me.

Returning to the fourth floor, I gaze long and hard down the hallway to make sure that the coast is clear before my second attempt on this coveted mattress. I hastily abscond with it and walk as fast as I can towards the exam room where I hid my gear. I didn't run, because I figured that would have appeared suspicious if I'd been caught, but, in hindsight, it's obvious that I looked suspicious enough to warrant arrest already—a barefoot, bedraggled idiot carrying a mattress through a deserted floor of a hospital in the middle of a Sunday night.

My things, like my conscience, remain undisturbed in the exam room. I borrow the delightful pillow from the patient's chair and make myself comfortable in my improvised bed on the floor. If anyone bursts in now, while I'm sleeping, I'll surely be caught. Reflecting, I giggle at the absurdity of this whole enterprise. I set my alarm on my cellular phone for five thirty, so that I can make it to the onramp as early as possible. In a matter of minutes, I'm zonked out, sleeping like the cows in the fields surrounding me, except that I'm well-sheltered, clean, and on a padded mattress. This Sabbath I gave God the chance to provide for me, and He provides for me in ways that I could never imagine.

Monday

My alarm wakes me at 0530 from sweet slumber. The day starts on a good note; I'm glad to hear my screeching alarm, instead of the harsh yell of a cop. I police up the area, leaving nothing but a bathtub ringed with dirt to hint at my stealthy conversion of this exam room into a hotel room. Anxious to avoid encounters with people in the hospital, I again use the fire escape, restoring my mattress to its former place in the hall. I descend into the food service area, and slide out of the building. The brisk and cool air of the predawn caresses my face, while the dewy grass brushes my feet. I sing vigorously, enjoying the nice morning as I merrily skip my way towards my destination.

Back on the same onramp where the drunk picked me up yesterday, I begin to ply my trade as the sun rises. A fruitless hour passes by and dampens my enthusiasm. At last, my first ride pulls over! Finally! Time to get the hell out of Podunkville, NC! I hop in the car to discover a single, grey haired lady who could have been my Grandmother. She takes off and tells me that she's only going as far as the next exit, the same one that the drunk dropped me off at yesterday! I force myself to act agreeable, and I tell her that's fine, because it was very considerate of her to pick me up, but inside I'm seething! She drops me off, and I once again walk the hateful miles back to the same onramp, to try my luck a third time. This mode of travel certainly has more than its share of delays and redundancies. I try to keep my head up as I walk and sweat under the rising sun.

A few minutes go by before a battered little truck pulls over on the onramp that's been playing yo-yo with me. The driver, a single young black male with cornrows, who looks like a scruffy, wannabe gangster says, "Wur ya off tuh, beeg daaawg?", and away we go. He reveals that he's only going a couple of exits down. Darn the luck. He drops me off at the exit 10 miles down from the hospital, the one that looked like it was dead center in the middle of nowhere on the map. I get off to discover that my impressions from the map were correct. There's nothing but a distant lone gas station.

Unsuccessfully, I stick out my thumb at the very sparse traffic on the onramp. Nothing. Hours go by. I laugh at myself for naively thinking that forty minutes was a long time to wait on Friday morning. Look at me now. This combination of events has kept me stuck in the general area of Podunkville, NC for nearly 24 hours. Eventually, I reach my limit. I give up. I'm through trying. I call my buddy Chris and ask him if he can detour to pick me up. I prop up a cardboard sign with the direction that I wish to travel, I lay down on my pack in the grass by the side of the asphalt, and I read my book, paying no attention to any traffic. I no longer care.

I'm literally not even three sentences into my book, when a car pulls over. I look at it curiously before I remember that I'm still hitching rides. I can't believe it. Just when I had lost all hope, this guy picks me up and takes me 80 miles down the road. He isn't going anywhere or doing anything; he just saw me sitting there, looking forlorn and stranded, and decided to help me out.

Once he drops me, I'm picked up by a carnival organizer, who offers me work as a carnie. I decline. If I wasn't in the

Army I would've tried it, just to see what it's like to be a carnie. After a couple more short rides, I land in a busy intersection with a group of bums, whose way of life consists of sitting by the roadside, holding cardboard signs, looking horrible, begging pity handouts from the traffic, and then spending that money on alcohol.

This intersection feels bad to me from the get go. I thumb the traffic, to no avail. I languish in a nearby gas station, which has seating and sells ice cream, thankfully. Again, I try my luck on the road. It looks like Lady Luck has forsaken me for good now. First, she seduced me with her ravishing good fortune on Friday, but she's plain tired of me now, and she's left me all alone. Now she will accompany some other poor devil, who will have the time of his life, if only for a short time. Maybe she went back to Vegas. Oh well, I can't take the time to mourn the wild whims of Lady Luck. I just got to deal with it.

The three bums rally up on the side of the road and head towards me. I discreetly shoulder my pack and feel a little apprehensive. However, I'm confident that I can outrun these old codgers, so I'm not worried. The youngest bum calls out, "Hey man, you want to take a break from the sun? We hang out in a little spot right here under these trees." I ponder his proposal. The blistering sun is killing me, and I don't feel like going right back to the gas station. I nod and follow the hoboes into their jungle.

A scene of utterly absolute fetid squalor confronts me in the bums' lair. The bums recline on an old padded blanket, whose original color can't be determined because it's so coated with filth. Several thousand cigarette butts litter the ground by the foot of the blanket. Just past that, hundreds of empty bottles of 40 oz malt liquor are piled haphazardly. Random pieces of trash and junk are scattered everywhere to complete the decorations. At first, the stink disgusts me, but after a little time I adjust to it, and it's not so bad. The whole place, bums included, could be a work of modern art. I can picture it in glass walls in a museum, with rich kids tapping on the windows and asking their Mommies, "Is that really how those people live?", and the Mommies gravely respond, "Yes, now isn't that terrible?"

These three skinny bums dress uniformly in filthy jeans and t-shirts. One is young, one middle aged, and the other old. They could almost be three generations of dirty tramps. Again, I've edited the conversation for content.

The oldest bum says, "Well come on in and have a seat man!

Make yourself at home! Don't worry, we ain't gonna do nothin' to ya."

I say, "Alright, don't mind if I do." The oldest bum pulls the cleanest piece of nearby cardboard over and offers me a seat. I take off my pack and recline in a similar posture as the bums. We introduce ourselves. They all shake hands firmly and respectably, like proper businessmen.

Tom says, "Do you want a drink? It's King Cobra, 'bout the cheapest stuff you can buy, but at least it's cold, and at least it's got alcohol in it."

I say, "Aw, no thanks man, none for me right now."

Tom says, "Suit yourself. So out there hitchhiking, huh?"

I say, "Yessir. Can't seem to get out of here though."

J.R. says, "Tell me about it man. I know what you mean. I've been hitchhiking for twenty years."

I say, "And how is it going for you?"

J.R. says, "Lousy!" It looks like it's been going lousy for J.R. A mass of horrific, ancient, sun burnt scars puff up on his face, most likely the ravages of some untreated skin disease. He spends a lot of time silent, just looking out at the horizon for something that nobody else seems to care about.

George says, "Yeah, 'ol J.R., he don't talk to much, but when he do, you better listen up. When he says somethin' it makes sense."

Tom says, "Yeah, unlike this guy George runnin' his mouth right now, he just rambles and mumbles about stupid stuff all day long."

George says, "Man, shut up before I smack you."

Tom says, "What you gonna do? I ain't skeered, old man!" George wallops Tom on the head with his open hand. They scuffle around a bit before Tom reconciles, saying, "Aw, you know I'm just messin' with you man. I love ya."

George chuckles and says, "Yeah I know. But anyway, as I was sayin' before I was so rudely interrupted, J.R. is a hell of a guy."

Tom, with much conviction, affirms George's statement, "Yer darn right. A hell of a guy." J.R. still stares morosely off into space, unconcerned. He knows they're talking about him, but he doesn't pay them any attention.

I say, "So how much can you guys pull in on an average day out there?"

Tom says, "Well, I come home with as much as fifty dollars, some days, like on a Friday maybe. You know Friday is payday, so that's the best day for it." I know that he's telling the truth.

And I also know now that those stories about panhandlers owning nice cars and homes are all lies. These men barely survive.

George says, "Yeah, it pays the bills, you know. Ha Ha!" Tom takes another swig out of the bottle and offers it to me again.

I say, "Well, you know what they say, when in Rome…" I take the bottle and heartily swig the cheap liquor. The tramps nod approvingly. It's not as bad as I had imagined. Like they said, at least it's cold, and at least it's alcoholic. When you're a bum, that's all that matters. I pass the bottle back around.

George says, "Say, did ya hear about that carnival going on down the road in town here?"

I say, "Actually I did, the organizer stopped by the side of the road and offered me a job. I told him no, because I'm trying to get back."

George says, "Huh. It's crap work anyway. Me and J.R. assembled a whole ride for them. They paid us in cash. I ain't bother to count the money or anything. Just stuffed it right in my pocket. Ain't no reason to count it when you know you'se getting cheated anyway. And there ain't a thing we could do about it either."

Tom says, "Look at you. Of course they cheated you."

George says, "What?"

Tom says, "Just look at yourself, you stinkin' bum!" George looks at his filthy jeans and disgustingly stained t shirt with the sleeves cut off. He examines his weathered skin and hoary hands.

George says, "Huh. Just look at you, man! You don't look no better!" This is a good point; they both appear quite haggard.

Tom says, "I look a lot better than you." George and Tom exchange sentimental blows with their fists upon each other's equally dirty bodies.

George says, "Aww man. I tell you dude, just last week I had five pair jeans, five t shirts, and ten pair socks. All brand new, all clean and nice. But the carnies, they ripped me off, man. They took all of it and kicked me out after me and J.R. built their ride."

Tom says, "That's the truth." I'm stumped for the right words to say. I don't know what George would do with all those clothes. What does he need them for? And why does he lament the loss of them? But we're all bums that way, and we all carry around things we don't need. The remembrance of the wrong done to him by the carnies darkens George's smiling face.

I say, "Man dude, that's a bummer."

George says, "Yeah, it was."

I say, "Well guys, I'm going to get back on the road to try my luck hitching again.

George stands up cordially and says, "Well it was nice to meet you, and good luck with it. Hope you get where you're tryin' to without too much trouble." This strikes me as a very polite and appropriate thing to say. What a simple and straightforward way to wish a wandering traveler off!

I say, "Thank ya'll kindly for the drink. I appreciate it."

Tom says, "Oh anytime. Have a good one."

I say, "Yep. You guys take it easy. I know you will." The hobo jungle retches me up into the waning sunlight. Strange worlds exist just beyond the realm of our senses. Before, I might have thought this place just a grove of natural foliage. Now I see it as the home of one very eccentric family, a family united by poverty and social status.

By the side of the road, the cars continue to pass. I bake in the sunlight. Like yesterday, the road dust clings to my feet and clothes. I'm nearly as grubby as the bums. I maintain my smile;

I try to keep smiling, because that's the only way I'll ever get picked up again. But still the cars pass. I'm tired. I know I'm finished, but I keep thumbing. I thumb until I don't even notice if I'm holding my hand the right way. Looking down, I see that my fingers curl strangely; I'm not even making the proper hitchhiking signal. It takes a conscious effort to give the thumbs up. I'm done. I retire to the air conditioned gas station and call my friend Chris to let him know where I am. He won't be through here until about 10:00, so I have a few hours to wait. I pull out my book and read for an hour.

I purchase a king size Snickers for dinner from the gas station. Outside, the last rays of the sun wave goodbye from behind another chain hotel. I sit on the bench in front of a closed service station, quietly observing and munching my candy bar. My new homeless friends wander on down the street aimlessly. Is that what it's like to be homeless? Cars continue to race every which way. With their lights on in the darkness, the vehicles transform into grotesque, inhuman monsters. They're all so busy, scurrying around like a bunch of callous cockroaches. The neon lights of some deep-fat fried grease fast food restaurant leer at me luridly. Glare from all the surrounding lights obscures the firmament as I gaze up into the heavens. I can't glimpse any stars; only a tepid gray color troubles my eyes.

This kills me. It all kills me. I can't stand it anymore. Inside, I'm quiet and still for the first time this weekend. I have nothing to do and nowhere to go. I'm just waiting, and I have a little more time to wait before this whole mad experiment is over. Just sitting on this bench, everything comes to a head and distresses me: the dismalness of the whole scene facing my eyes, the unhealthy candy and junk food, the bums' tormented lifestyle, Michelle's Lithium, all those people who turn their heads so they don't have to look at me on the side of the road, all the traffic, all the consumption. It's so hectic, and yet so vacuous. Is this America? Is this freedom? Is this what people give their lives for? Is this the dream that we all strive for? It breaks my heart. I'm sitting alone, with people in glass and metal bubbles all around me, and I start crying. The tears slide out silently and easily. This is the most unwholesome, and yet the most common vision of America for me.

Birds flutter from atop a nearby rooftop. A whole formation of them flies in a dance with the twilight. With boundless energy, they loop and soar through the air. They follow each other, fifty creatures moving as a single unit.

Watching them reassures me, and puts me in a prayerful mood. I pray silently, emptying my mind and turning towards God as best as I know how, just like the birds, which fly for God as best as they know how.

The darkness drives me back inside the gas station to finish my book. Fortunately, my book engrosses me, so the hours fly by. Periodically, I look up to observe the various people hanging around a gas station in the middle of the night. They all look like villains. Of course, I probably look like quite a strange fiend myself. Across the table from me an extremely old, withered man, dressed in forty year old clothing, has fallen asleep over a bottle of milk. He snores and drools all over the table. I wake him up and ask if he's all right. He grunts, nods, buys another bottle of milk, and then, once again, plants himself on the seat.

I finish the book my Mother gave me, a depressing picture of life in modern Afghanistan, written from a Scandinavian feminist's perspective. Now I have to sit and wait for Chris; he should be here soon. Worthless trash fills the gas station shelves. Cookies, razors, candy, soda, prophylactics, pills, magazines, and potato chips all jostle for space and upset my eyes with their gaudy advertising. It's all highly processed, preserved, made in China type plastic junk, even the food. The food is just high fructose corn syrup and salt in different forms. Nothing in here is real, natural, or wholesome. I'm no health nut, but the products of the gas station sicken me, because, to me, they have become a metaphor for accepting the fake, rather than demanding the real.

Chris walks through the door, instantly lifting my gloomy spirits. I'm so ecstatic to see him; I'm finally out of this mess! I will make it back without missing accountability formation! Grinning from ear to ear, I hug my rescuer. We leave the gas station and drive the two hours back to the base. Chris listens incredulously as I recount my shenanigans. My car waits on the highway near the base. I drive it in and arrive at the barracks at 12:30 AM, so I made it back with five hours to spare. Incidentally, my alarm fails to wake me Tuesday morning, so I miss formation, and I'm counted as not present anyway. Oh well.

Conclusion

So that was my weekend, pretty much the most random, ridiculous weekend of my whole life. But I enjoyed it very much. I feel like I packed a whole year of normal life experience into just four days, because it was so intense. It felt fantastic to go out and do something extraordinary. This is what can happen when you decide to really go with the flow, rafting solo down the fluctuating river of traffic. The rapids will terrify and titillate you, the backwaters will bore you, the scenery will amaze you, and the wildlife...can be pretty wild. Overall, I believe that only the best people in the world picked me up. Everyone was nice, and I never once felt threatened or uncomfortable.

Tuesday, I gave Michelle a buzz to let her know that I made it back ok. I plan on visiting Asheville again on the next four day weekend, and this time I'll drive my car and bring a companion to join in on the revelry.

I called up John, my first ride, to take him up on his offer of a beer. On the phone he invited me to go kayaking at his beach house, and to go camping at a nearby nudist colony. I was down for it all, but he didn't seem so keen on it after I made it clear to him that I'm definitely not a homosexual. Still, he was polite and enthusiastic about my adventure.

Yesterday I ordered a book, "How to hitch rides on other people's yachts". That sounds like a pretty decent way to see the world. I've done my time as a soldier, why not try sailor now?

My time in the Army continues slowly ticking away. I'm nine months out right now, which means I'm pregnant with freedom! I can feel that bright little seed of hope growing inside of me, and I'm anticipating it like a slavering, writhing puppy waiting for chow, jumping up and down and wagging his tail so hard it shakes his whole body. When that day comes, it will be like a thousand Christmases; I might have to dance an ecstatic jig at my final military formation. Thanks Uncle Sam, as tough as it's been for me to conform, you prepared me to appreciate my independence.

CPSIA information can be obtained at www.ICGtesting.com
Printed in the USA
LVOW120901040112

262329LV00002B/222/P